*For Josh Hughes who really
knows about robots
I.W.*

*For Martin
A.R.*

PUFFIN BOOKS

Published by the Penguin Group
Penguin Books Ltd, 80 Strand, London WC2R 0RL, England
Penguin Group (USA), Inc., 375 Hudson Street, New York, New York 10014, USA
Penguin Books Australia Ltd, 250 Camberwell Road, Camberwell, Victoria 3124, Australia
Penguin Books Canada Ltd, 10 Alcorn Avenue, Toronto, Ontario, Canada M4V 3B2
Penguin Books India (P) Ltd, 11 Community Centre, Panchsheel Park, New Delhi – 110 017, India
Penguin Group (NZ), cnr Airborne and Rosedale Roads, Albany, Auckland 1310, New Zealand
Penguin Books (South Africa) (Pty) Ltd, 24 Sturdee Avenue, Rosebank 2196, South Africa

Penguin Books Ltd, Registered Offices: 80 Strand, London WC2R 0RL, England

www.penguin.com

First published in hardback by David & Charles Children's Books 2000
First published in paperback by Gullane Children's Books 2001
First published in Puffin Books 2003
9 10 8

Text copyright © Ian Whybrow, 2000
Illustrations copyright © Adrian Reynolds, 2000
All rights reserved

The moral right of the author and illustrator has been asserted

Manufactured in China

British Library Cataloguing in Publication Data
A CIP catalogue record for this book is available from the British Library

ISBN-13: 978-0-14056-982-7
ISBN-10: 0-14056-982-0

This
Harry
book belongs to

. . . .

Harry
and the
Robots

Ian Whybrow and Adrian Reynolds

PUFFIN

It was a shock for Harry
when his robot fell over.
It was just doing a nice march
and suddenly its lights went out.

Harry heard Nan coughing in the yard,
so he ran out to show her.

Some of the robot's batteries had leaked onto its wires.
They put him in a parcel and sent him to the robot hospital.
"They'll know how to mend him," Nan said.

Harry wanted to make another robot to play with while he
waited for his marching robot to come back.
Nan said, "Good idea. We'll use my best scissors if you like."
They laid the things ready on the table.

But they never got started.
Mum made Nan go to bed,
her cough was so bad.

When Harry woke up the next morning, there was no Nan. The ambulance had come in the night. She had to go into hospital, Mum said, for her bad chest.

That day, Sam watched
TV a lot.

Harry started making a robot all by himself.
He wanted to use Nan's best scissors. Nan had said he could.
But Sam said, "No! Those are Nan's!"

That was why Harry threw his Stegosaurus at her.

Mum took him to settle down.
She said he could use Nan's best scissors if
Nan had said so, but only while she was
watching. He had to be very careful
though, because they were sharp.

Harry worked hard
all morning . . .

. . . until there was a new robot. A special one.
    Harry taught it marching. He taught it talking.
    But most of all he taught it blasting.
The robot said,
"Ha - Lo Har - Ree.
Have - you - got - a - cough?
BLAAAST!"

The hospital was big but they found Nan in there.

Mum said Sam and Harry had
to wait outside Nan's room.
They waved through the window
but Nan did not open her eyes.

Sam and Mum whispered with the doctor. So Harry
slipped into the room – just him and the special robot.

He put the special robot by Nan.
The robot said,
    "Ha - Lo - Nan.
        Have - you - got - a - cough?"
She opened one eye. It winked.
The robot said,
    "I - will - blast - your - cough.
        BLAAAST!"

That was when Mum ran in saying – "Harry! No!"
But the doctor said not to worry, it was fine.
A robot would be a nice helper for Nan.

That evening, Harry was very busy.

He joined . . .

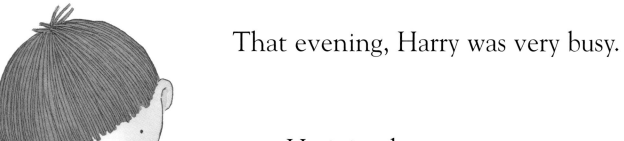

he stuck . . .

he painted and . . .

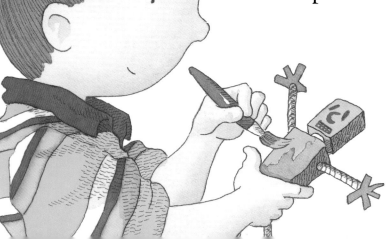

Harry made five more
special robots to look
after Nan.

The robots guarded Nan.
They marched for her.
They blasted her cough.
And soon she was better.

Nan came home and unpacked her things.
"You're a good looker-afterer," she whispered.
"And my special robots," said Harry.
"Oh yes, them too," said Nan.
"I'd like to keep them by me, do you mind?"
Harry did not mind at all.

Nan went out into the yard to see how
the chickens were getting on.
They were just fine.

That afternoon a parcel arrived. It was the marching robot,
back from the robot hospital. His light went on
and he did a nice march – good as new.

Look out for all of Harry's adventures!

ISBN 0140569804

Harry and the Bucketful of Dinosaurs
Harry finds some old, plastic dinosaurs and cleans them, finds out their names and takes them everywhere with him – until, one day, they get lost... Will he ever find them?

Harry and the Snow King
There's just enough snow for Harry to build a very small snow king. But then the snow king disappears – who's kidnapped him?

ISBN 0140569863

ISBN 0140569820

Harry and the Robots
Harry's robot is sent to the toy hospital to be fixed, so Harry and Nan decide to make a new one. When Nan has to go to hospital, Harry knows just how to help her get better!

Harry and the Dinosaurs say "Raahh!"
Harry's dinosaurs are acting strangely. They're hiding all over the house, refusing to come out... Could it be because today is the day of Harry's dentist appointment?

ISBN 0140569812

ISBN 0140569847

Harry and the Dinosaurs Romp in the Swamp
Harry has to play at Charlie's house and doesn't want to share his dinosaurs. But when Charlie builds a fantastic swamp, Harry and the dinosaurs can't help but join in the fun!

Harry and the Dinosaurs make a Christmas Wish
Harry and the dinosaurs would *love* to own a duckling. They wait till Christmas and make a special wish, but Santa leaves them something even more exciting...!

ISBN 0141380179 (hbk)
ISBN 0140569529 (pbk)

ISBN 0140569839

ISBN 0140569855

Harry and the Dinosaurs play Hide-and-Seek
Harry and the Dinosaurs have a Very Busy Day
Join in with Harry and his dinosaurs for some peep-through fold-out fun! These exciting books about shapes and colours make learning easy!